Guest Spot

Playalong for Clarinet

TODAY'S BIGGEST HITS

GW00481314

Wise Publications
part of The Music Sales Group

London / New York / Paris / Sydney / Copenhagen / Berlin / Madrid / Hong Kong / Tokyo

Published by
Wise Publications
14-15 Berners Street, London W1T 3LJ, UK.

Exclusive Distributors:
Music Sales Limited
Distribution Centre, Newmarket Road,
Bury St Edmunds, Suffolk IP33 3YB, UK.
Music Sales Pty Limited
Units 3-4, 17 Willfox Street, Condell Park,
NSW 2200, Australia.

Order No. AM1007985
ISBN: 978-1-78305-400-8
This book © Copyright 2013 Wise Publications,
a division of Music Sales Limited.

Arrangements by Christopher Hussey.
Backing tracks by Jeremy Birchall & Christopher Hussey.
Clarinet played by Howard McGill.
CD recorded, mixed and mastered by Jonas Persson.
Printed in the EU.

Your Guarantee of Quality:
As publishers, we strive to produce every book to
the highest commercial standards.
The music has been freshly engraved and the book has been
carefully designed to minimise awkward page turns and
to make playing from it a real pleasure.
Particular care has been given to specifying acid-free, neutral-sized
paper made from pulps which have not been elemental chlorine bleached.
This pulp is from farmed sustainable forests and was
produced with special regard for the environment.
Throughout, the printing and binding have been planned to
ensure a sturdy, attractive publication which should give years of enjoyment.
If your copy fails to meet our high standards,
please inform us and we will gladly replace it.

www.musicsales.com

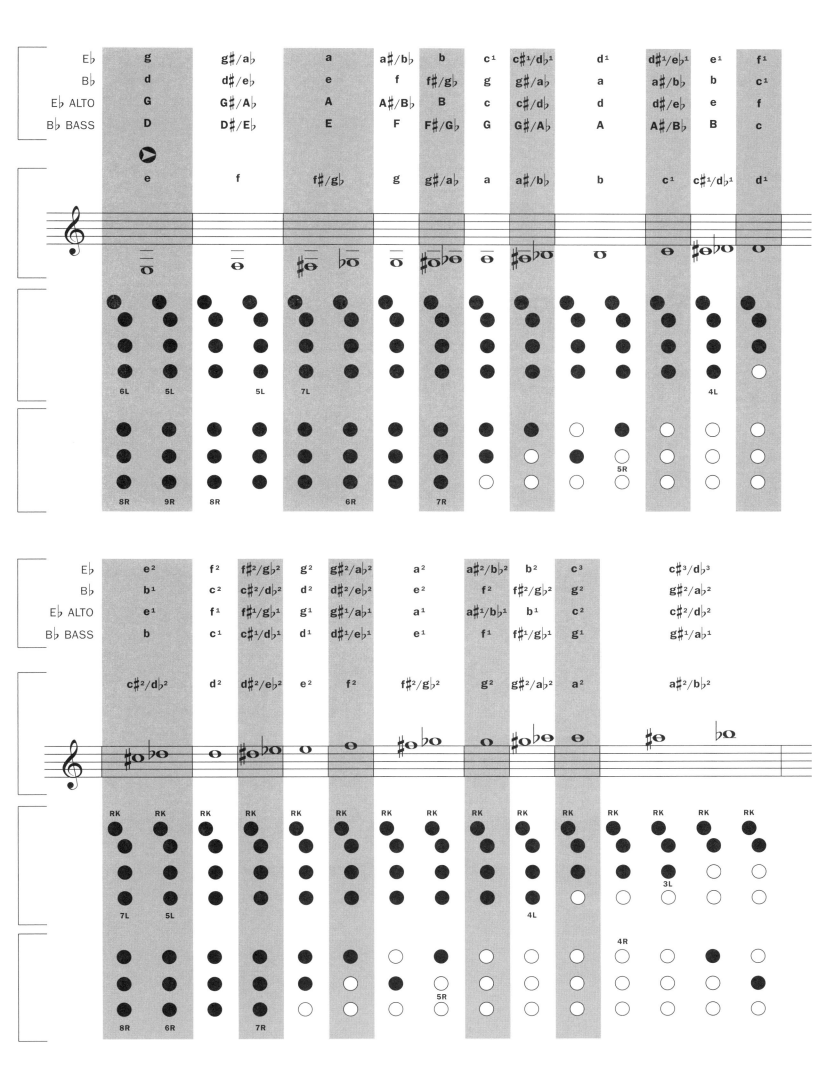

Indicates the lower limit of the best playing range for E♭, B♭, E♭ Alto and B♭ Bass Clarinets

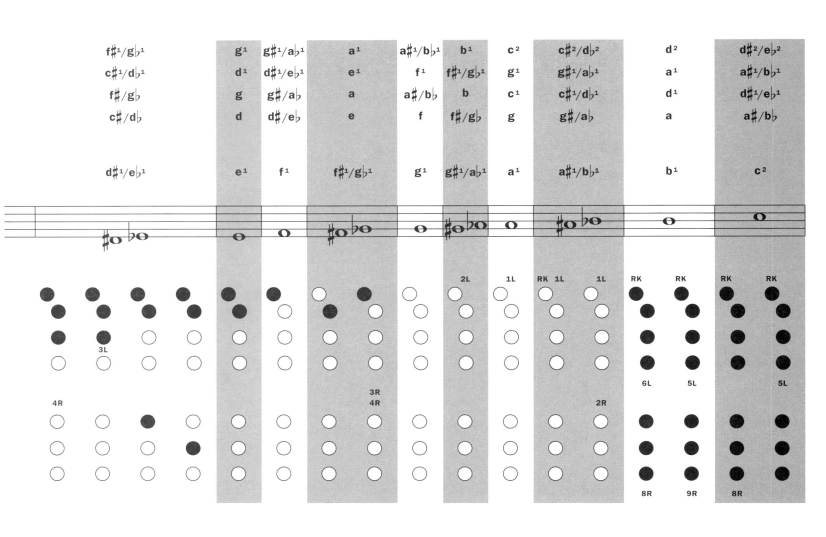

Fingering Chart

Indicates the upper limit of the best playing range for E♭ and B♭ Clarinets

Indicates the upper limit of the best playing range for E♭ Alto and B♭ Bass Clarinet

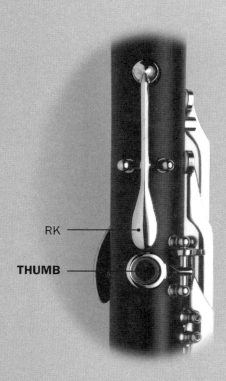

RK

THUMB

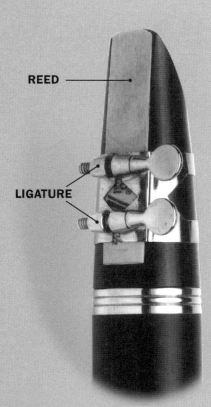

REED

LIGATURE

Mouthpiece

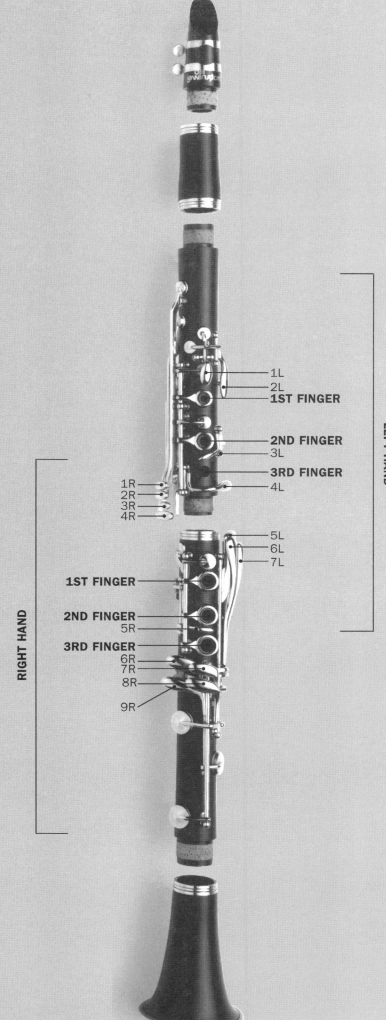

1L
2L
1ST FINGER

2ND FINGER
3L

3RD FINGER

1R
2R
3R
4R

4L

LEFT HAND

5L
6L
7L

1ST FINGER

2ND FINGER
5R

RIGHT HAND

3RD FINGER
6R
7R
8R

9R

Guest Spot

22 (Taylor Swift)

Words & Music by Taylor Swift, Max Martin & Johan Schuster

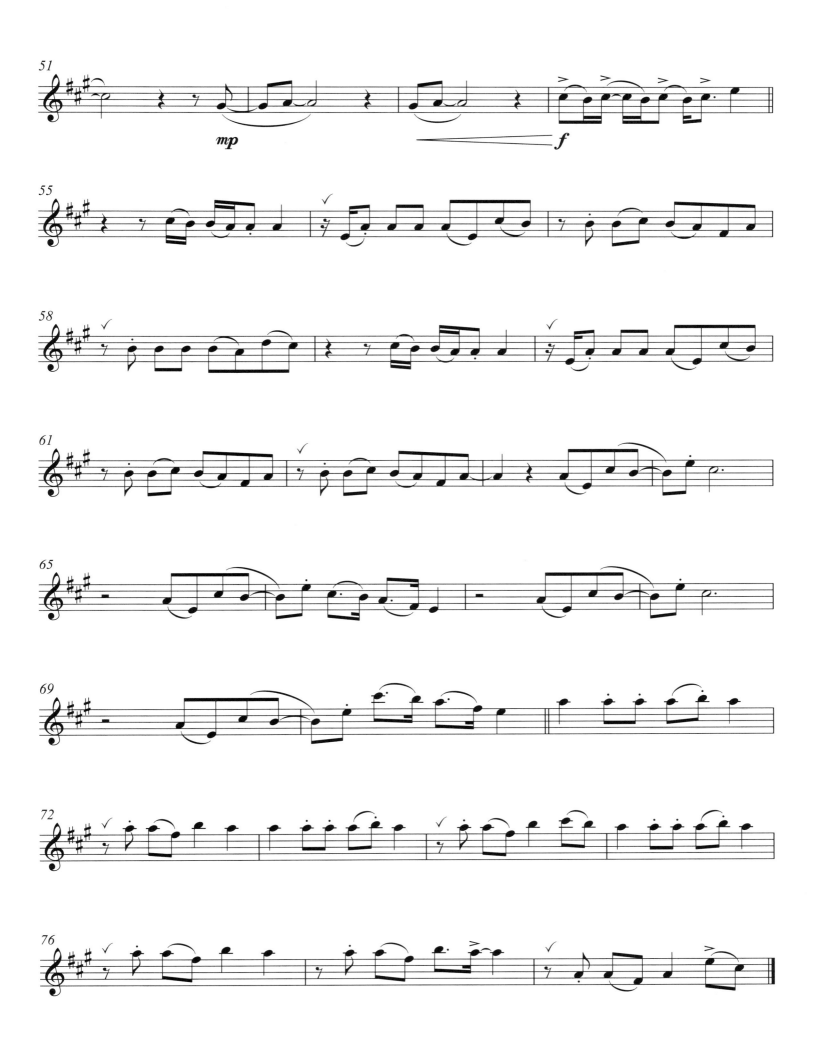

9

Best Song Ever (One Direction)

Words & Music by Wayne Hector, John Ryan, Julian Bunetta & Edward Drewett

Big When I Was Little (Eliza Doolittle)

Words & Music by Wayne Hector, Stephen Robson, Ervan Coleman & Eliza Sophie Caird

to Coda ⊕

D.S. al Coda   ⊕ Coda

Hey Porsche (Nelly)

Words & Music by Cornell Haynes, Justin Franks, David Glass, Breyan Isaac & Harrison Kipner

Rhythmically ♩ = 116

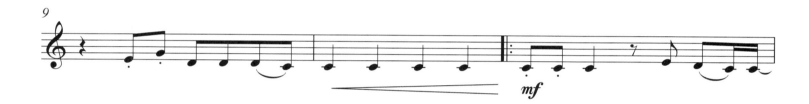

Just Give Me A Reason (Pink)

Words & Music by Alecia Moore, Jeff Bhasker & Nate Ruess

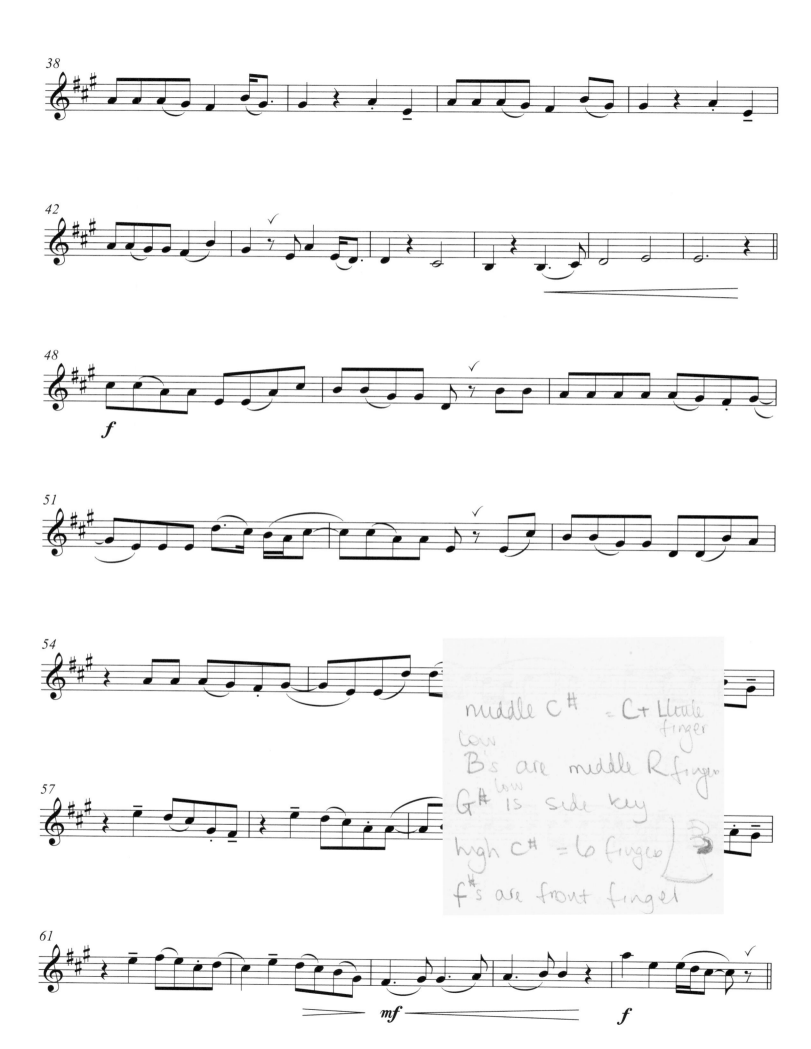

Let Her Go (Passenger)

Words & Music by Michael Rosenberg

Right Place Right Time (Olly Murs)

Words & Music by Stephen Robson, Claude Kelly & Oliver Murs

Smoothly, with expression ♩ = 140

Panic Cord (Gabrielle Aplin)

Words & Music by Jez Ashurst, Gabrielle Aplin & Nicholas Atkinson

Steadily, with a bounce ♩ = 106

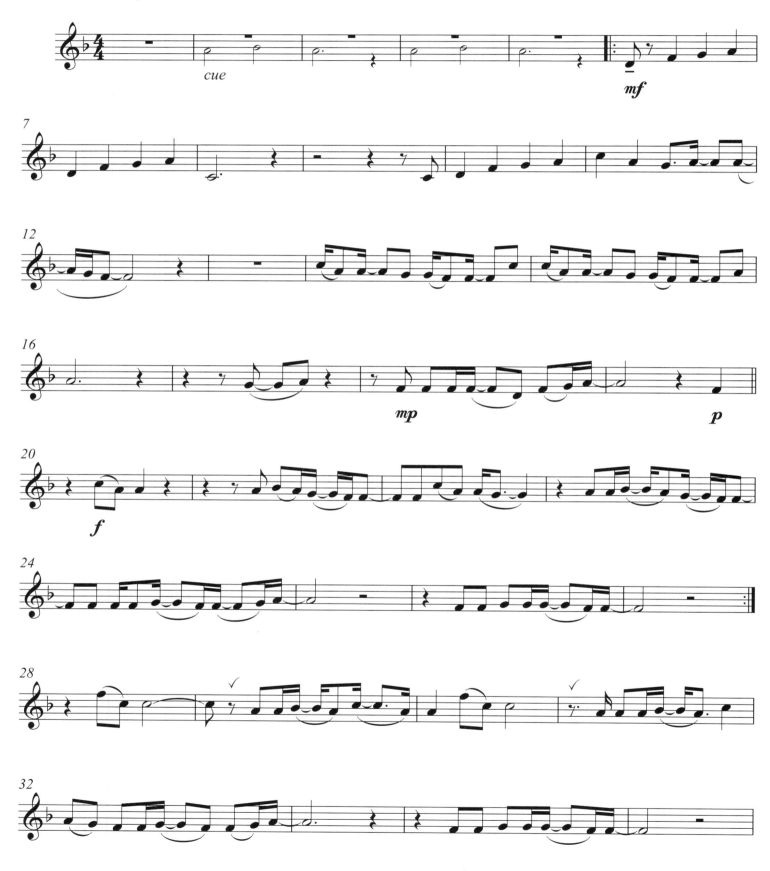

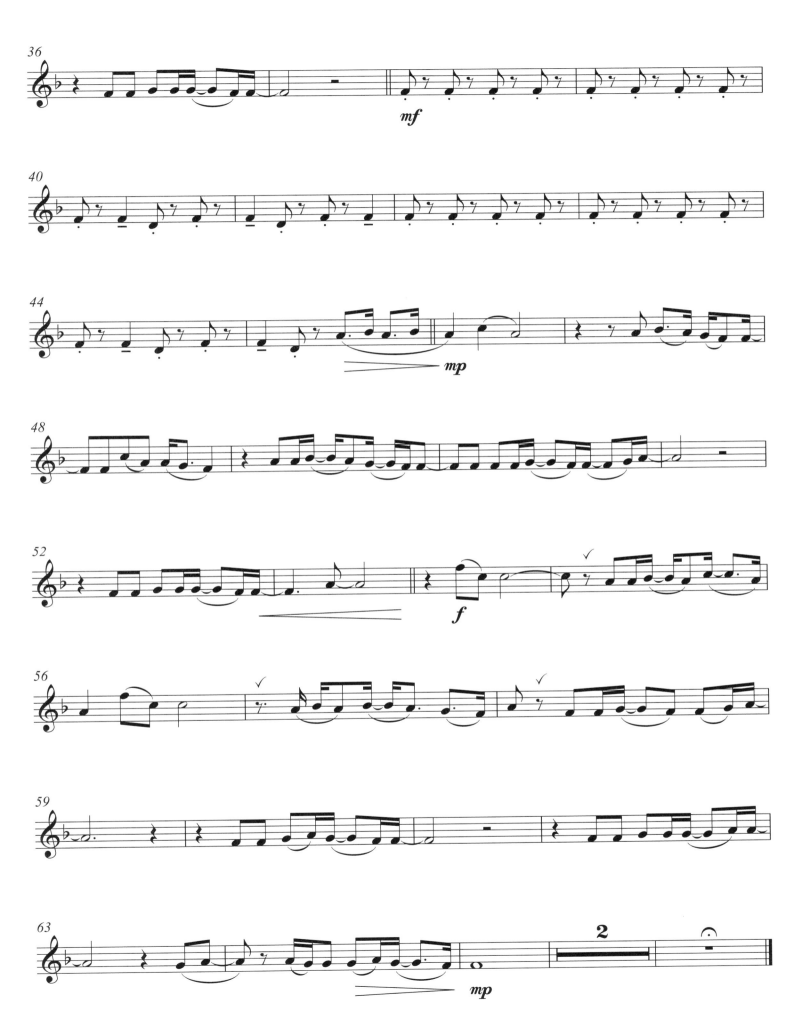

Stay (Rihanna, featuring Mikky Ekko)

Words & Music by Justin Parker & Mikky Ekko

Walks Like Rihanna (The Wanted)

Words & Music by Andrew Hill, Lukasz Gottwald, Henry Russell Walter, Edvard Erfjord & Henrik Michelsen

Brightly and smoothly ♩ = 126

CD Track Listing

Full instrumental performances...

1. Tuning notes

2. 22
(Swift/Martin/Schuster) Sony/ATV Music Publishing (UK) Limited/
Kobalt Music Publishing Limited

3. Best Song Ever
(Hector/Ryan/Bunetta/Drewett) Warner/Chappell Music Publishing Limited/
Universal/MCA Music Limited/Copyright Control

4. Big When I Was Little
(Hector/Robson/Coleman/Caird) Universal Music Publishing Limited/
Imagem Music/Warner/Chappell Music Publishing Limited

5. Hey Porsche
(Haynes/Franks/Glass/Isaac/Kipner) Kobalt Music Publishing Limited/
Warner/Chappell North America Limited/Sony/ATV Music Publishing/
BMG Rights Management (UK) Limited

6. Just Give Me A Reason
(Moore/Bhasker/Ruess) EMI Music Publishing Limited/Sony/ATV Music Publishing/
Warner/Chappell North America Limited

7. Let Her Go
(Rosenberg) Sony/ATV Music Publishing (UK) Limited

8. Panic Cord
(Ashurst/Aplin/Atkinson) Universal Music Publishing Limited/
BMG Rights Management (UK) Limited/Stage Three Music Publishing Limited

9. Right Place Right Time
(Robson/Kelly/Murs) Universal Music Publishing Limited/Imagem Music/
Warner/Chappell North America Limited

10. Stay
(Parker/Ekko) Sony/ATV Music Publishing (UK) Limited

11. Walks Like Rihanna
(Hill/Gottwald/Walter/Erfjord/Michelsen) Kobalt Music Publishing Limited/
Nettwerk One Music Limited

Backing tracks only...

12. 22
13. Best Song Ever
14. Big When I Was Little
15. Hey Porsche
16. Just Give Me A Reason
17. Let Her Go
18. Panic Cord
19. Right Place Right Time
20. Stay
21. Walks Like Rihanna

To remove your CD from the plastic sleeve,
lift the small lip to break the perforations.
Replace the disc after use for convenient storage